TARTAN HOUSE

THE 13TH FLOOR

by Scott R. Welvaert

www.12StoryLibrary.com

12-Story Library is an imprint of Peterson Publishing Company and Press Room Editions.

Produced for 12-Story Library by Red Line Editorial

Photographs ©: Shutterstock Images, cover, 3

Cover Design: Jake Nordby

ISBN
978-1-63235-056-5 (hardcover)
978-1-63235-116-6 (paperback)
978-1-62143-097-1 (hosted ebook)

Library of Congress Control Number: 2014946008

Printed in the United States of America
Mankato, MN
October, 2014

CHAPTER
1

Sam Wentworth hated moving. Really hated it. But he had no other choice. Ever since his mother died 11 years ago, he felt the need to support his father's career, which sometimes dragged them across the country. At least this time his father had landed his dream job—chief financial officer of a networking firm. And Sam didn't want to wreck that. Plus, it wasn't like Sam hadn't done this before. Over the years, he'd actually gotten pretty good at moving to a new school and fitting in.

Sam roughly stuffed his bag and coat inside his locker, mentally preparing himself for another first day of school.

"Army brat or executive minion?"

Sam peeked around his locker door at the girl two doors down. Cute with a brown braid in her hair. She looked like a tomboy in her jeans, combat boots, and flannel shirt.

"Excuse me?" he said.

Crouched and rummaging in her locker, she said, "There are three types of new students: first timers, army brats, and executive minions. My money is on minion." She gathered her books and stood up.

Sam shut his locker. "What makes you say that?"

"First timers come into a new school with cow eyes. They have no clue what's going on, but you look like you've done this before."

She stepped toward him. Poked at his shirt.

"Hollister shirt. Rocawear jeans. And practically glowing Nikes. You're an executive minion if I ever saw one."

Sam frowned. "What if I told you I was an army brat?"

The girl blew a stray strand of hair out of her face. "Then you'd be a liar, and a bad one too."

Sam couldn't help but smile. "How would you know?"

"Because I'm an army brat. I know a thing or two about scoping out a situation."

"Figures," Sam said. He extended his hand to her. "Sam Wentworth."

She shook his hand. "Liz Fallon." Then she reached out and touched the spiked skull medallion dangling from his neck. "I'm sure you'll fit in just fine."

Sam watched her disappear in the crowded halls. No problem. Just another move. Just another city. He had this covered. He shut his locker and headed to homeroom.

Sam took a seat at one of the tables in Mr. Hoffstatler's classroom. Other students slowly rolled in. Three guys wearing letterman jackets laughed as they entered. Obviously football players. The biggest one of them snuck a look at

Sam and spied the glint of steel hanging around his neck.

"Guys!" he yelled across the classroom. "We got another playa!"

They all sat at Sam's table. They wore the same necklace, a sterling silver chain with a spiked skull medallion, purchased from the *Warpath* video game website.

"What's your *Warpath* tag, bro?" the big one asked.

"HAZMAT," Sam said, surprised that football players had taken an interest in him.

The middle one laughed. "Sweet. I'm Austin Taylor. Middle linebacker." He pointed to his tall, thin friend. "This is Johnny Keller. Wide receiver." Then he pointed to the big dude, almost 300 pounds. "And this is Edward Jackson. Left tackle, but we all call him Mack. We're members of clan BLITZN."

Warpath was Sam's favorite game, a first-person combat shooter with an array of modern military weapons. He had logged hundreds of hours over the summer.

"Play a lot of video games?" Sam asked.

Johnny piped up. "Yeah, usually first-person shooters, but Austin also likes the scary horror ones."

"Just wait until you see the new game I'm trying to get my hands on," Austin said. "It's been banned—"

"Alright, alright, alright," Mr. Hoffstatler interrupted. "Sit down and pipe down. Let's get this over with so that you all can get to first period. First, there's a pep fest on Friday for the game. The drama club is opening auditions for the fall musical."

Sam checked his phone as their teacher droned on.

"Finally," he said, "remember the Matty Dellapest Rule—we have a zero-tolerance policy. The school prohibits violence and all forms of bullying."

"Who's Matty Dellapest?" Sam whispered to his new friends.

Austin answered, "Some geek fifteen years ago got bullied. He got a little tweaked. A bunch of kids got busted."

"It must have been bad," Sam said.

Johnny laughed. "Nah. The school just has to cover themselves."

CHAPTER
2

"Dad!" Sam yelled. "Pizza's here!"

Sam brought the pizza to the table and set out a couple of plates and napkins. He was well into his second slice before his dad joined him.

"How was the first day?" Sam asked.

Sam swallowed his pizza. "Okay."

"Good," his dad said, taking a step back toward his den.

"This guy Austin is having a gamer party this weekend. Can I go?"

His father took a deep breath, pained to have to pause for conversation. "Sure," was all he said.

Sam frowned. He missed his mom at dinner the most. At least she had stayed to talk. Sam looked across the table to his father's empty chair. The room was eerily quiet.

He ate three slices, closed the box, and put the rest of the pizza in the fridge. Dinner for tomorrow night. Then he shuffled down the basement stairs to the family room, fired up his game system, and logged in. Half the reason Sam escaped to video games was to bring noise into his life. He couldn't stand the quiet. The silence. His mom gone. His dad off tending to his work. Just Sam. All alone.

With his headset on and active, he launched *Warpath*. His system searched for players online.

A blinking cursor alerted him to three new notifications on his profile. Sam's new friends from homeroom had sent him invites. He accepted, and a chat screen popped open.

MLBmayh3m joined the chat.
Austin Taylor.

JohnnyDeeperWR joined the chat.
Johnny Keller.

Finally monsterMack joined the chat.
Edward Jackson.

"Noob," Austin yelled, "Ready to kick
some butt?"

"Um, sure," Sam said, adjusting the
microphone on his headset.

"You don't sound so sure," Johnny chimed
in. "You're not going to wimp out on us?"

Sam really wasn't into trash talking online.
He muted most people he played with. But he
was new to town, so he didn't want be the odd
one out.

"Shut your face. I'd like to see what you can
do on the battlefield," he said.

Mack chimed in. "Big talk, noob."

They agreed to battle another clan. A war
map popped up. The countdown began.

"Warehouse?" Austin said. "I hate
this map."

"Lots of nooks and crannies to hide in," Sam said.

The timer expired and all their online characters moved out.

"Go, go, go!" Johnny yelled.

Sam maneuvered his avatar in and out of shadows. Someone fired at him from an aisle. Sam switched to thermal optics, and his target lit up in white. He fired. A kill, 100 points.

Austin whistled. "Ooh, look at the noob go!"

Sam's headphones erupted with the sounds of gunfire. Frag grenades exploded. Points tallied.

From across the map, Johnny's character was hit with shrapnel. "Aw, man. I'm gonna get him back!" he cursed.

A volley of submachine gunfire rattled through the speakers. Austin cackled. "What idiots! I just aced like seven in a row."

Onscreen, Mack's character ran past Sam's. "Watch this," Sam heard in his headset.

Sam's character turned around. Mack's avatar ran circles around an enemy. The enemy spun around and fired randomly. Mack laughed wildly over the system.

"Dude, you suck!" He finished the mockery by blasting the guy from behind. "Booyah!"

All throughout the match, Sam felt a black pit in his stomach grow as he played with his new friends. The trash talk. The cursing. The poking fun at all the other players. But at the same time, Sam didn't want them to not like him. He'd never had friends on the football team before. At every other school, the football players were the kings of cool. Girls. Parties. Everything. Sam wanted that. So he continued playing all night, match after match. He racked up kill-streak points and watched all his new friends poke fun, ridicule, and belittle other players. After more than two dozen games, it became easier to ignore their comments. Sometimes he even found himself laughing along with them.

CHAPTER
3

The crowd at Steinbeck Senior High Stadium roared. Austin Taylor had blitzed right up the gut and sacked the quarterback. He pumped his fist to the night sky. The defense trotted off the field for the punt. Sam sat in the first row nibbling on his popcorn. He'd never really liked football, but he liked hearing the roar of the crowd. Anything but silence. Johnny ran onto the field to receive the punt. On the bench, Mack turned around and found Sam.

"Hazmat!" he yelled.

Sam raised his fist in acknowledgement. It felt weird, but he figured he had to show some kind of team spirit or whatever.

"Jeez, one week in and you're partying with the football team," Liz said.

Sam turned toward the sound of her voice.

"I have this weird way of making friends," Sam replied.

"Just be careful with those guys, okay?" she said as she walked by and sat down with some of her friends.

"Yeah, sure."

The crowd roared. Sam turned back to the game to see what had happened. Johnny had returned the punt for a touchdown.

✦ ✦ ✦ ✦ ✦

After the game, Sam walked over to Austin's house. He rang the doorbell and Austin's mom answered.

"They're downstairs," she said. "We have pizza and soda in the kitchen. Make a plate and head on down."

"Thanks."

Sam hung up his coat and grabbed some pizza. He was met with a wave of laughter as he walked down the stairs. On a mega-huge television played a compilation video of Austin's *Warpath* escapades, complete with his own zany narration. Around the basement, football players and friends crowded on couches and peered over shoulders, laughing at the onscreen antics.

"Hazmat!" Austin yelled. "Get a load of these idiots!"

Sam sat down on the sofa and watched. The video called out numerous gamers online, showing their gamer tags onscreen as Austin toyed with them. One player ran away from him as Austin shot him with a grenade launcher, sending the soldier sky-high.

"Loser!" Austin's voice-over taunted. The basement erupted in laughter.

Sam ate his pizza and drank his soda.

The next montage began. Austin took up position at the end of a bottleneck and sniped two players as they funneled their way through. "What idiots," Austin called out in his narration.

Mack pointed at the screen, where a list of gamer tags identified the players Austin mowed down. "Is that Sebastian and Harry, the glee club geeks?"

"Yep."

The room exploded with laughter.

Fast footsteps thundered down the stairs and stopped the celebration. A tall, lanky guy with a devilish smile on his face emerged from the stairwell.

Austin stood up and said, "Tater! Did you get it?"

Tater reached underneath the front of his coat and pulled out a clear plastic case. "Of course I got it."

Sam looked at the game in Tater's hands. It didn't have any artwork or branding. It was simply a clear case with a blank disc.

Austin held up the disc. "They won't even sell this here. That's how freakadelic it is! It's a crime to play this game, dudes! A crime!"

Confused murmurs floated through the crowd.

Austin took the case and kissed it. "Buckle up, kiddos. This is the game that's been burning up the Internet. *The 13th Floor.* Banned in all the states for violence, gore, and horror. It's the scariest thing ever programmed."

Austin stepped over to his gaming system and slid in the disc. The screen went to black. The gaming console went through a series of hums and shuddered. A high-pitched squeal streamed through the speakers.

"Pardon me," an old, mysterious voice said on the television. "Some adjustments need to be made."

The blackness on the screen grew lighter. Everyone leaned forward, squinting to make out the image pushing through the shadows. A hint of a masked face began to emerge. Sam could make out big black goggles over a white porcelain mask with a large beak, like a stork. The face looked to the left, then the right. In the darkness behind it, water dripped, echoing as if they were standing in a large, cavernous room.

"I am the doctor," the voice said. "And I've seen all your minds. Your innermost fears. Your lies. The blackness that slides across your souls."

Behind the ominous face came the faint sounds of a chain being dragged across a tile floor. A scream. A knife slicing into something.

"This game is quite simple. Find me before you go insane."

The basement lights flickered. A *pop* was felt through the entire house as the electricity went out. The room was plummeted into darkness, but the doctor's faint profile remained on the screen. Everyone around Sam gasped.

From upstairs, Austin's parents swore. Their murmuring voices sounded panicked. Onscreen, the doctor turned around and walked away into the darkness, his footsteps scuffing the tile floor as he disappeared.

The lights abruptly turned back on. Austin's mom called down, "What are you doing down there?"

Austin appeared embarrassed, but he covered it up quickly by running a hand though his hair.

"Nothing, Mom. Just playing a game."

"Well, be careful. The power just switched off."

"I know, Mom."

Everyone at the party looked at each other. Faces that had been flushed with excitement just a few minutes ago were now pale and pinched.

Johnny broke the silence. "That was so sick! I got dibs!" He grabbed the controller and jumped onto the couch.

Sam had never seen a game like it. Drenched in shadows, the player could interact with almost everything in the environment. And the environment was riveting. A sanitarium check-in desk covered in papers. Lightbulbs flickering on and off, casting eerie shadows everywhere. Blood smeared on the floors.

Johnny's character walked up to the desk and opened the drawers. Checked the contents. Read a clipboard of papers that chronicled a recent death in the sanitarium.

"Weird," Johnny said.

After inspecting the front desk, he walked down a hallway. On the walls, the phrase "Don't find the doctor," was written in blood. The floor was flooded. A burst pipe dripped from the ceiling next to a nearby bathroom. Johnny entered the bathroom. Five stalls stood before him, all of the doors closed. He stepped forward and opened the first one. Nothing except a broken toilet. He moved on to the second one. Nothing. He slowly opened each door, but all of the stalls were empty.

"What the——?" Johnny said.

When he turned his character around, the doctor stood behind him.

Sam didn't know what frightened him more, the sudden appearance of the doctor or the gasps of everyone around him.

Onscreen, the doctor stabbed Johnny's character. The screen grew fuzzy. The character collapsed. Darkness shrouded the screen as the doctor said, "You didn't think this would be easy, did you?"

CHAPTER
4

The doctor's voice echoed in Sam's mind. "You didn't think this would be easy, did you?"

The game had gotten in his head. He couldn't understand it. He had watched countless scary movies. But that long-beaked mask and those goggles haunted him. Even the sounds from the game were still rattling through his ears. The shadowy lighting, the hazy images— all of it felt scored permanently into his brain.

Sam rubbed his head and got out of bed. It was Monday morning. He needed to get ready for school. The house around him was still. Silent. He showered, brushed his teeth, and got dressed. Walking downstairs, he passed their family portrait but averted his eyes. He never looked at the pictures of his mom anymore. It always made him sad.

Sam ate his cereal alone at the kitchen table. His father always went to work early in the morning and came home late. It was probably his way of dealing with the death of his wife, but it still sucked for Sam, eating another meal alone.

✦ ✦ ✦ ✦ ✦

At school, Sam sorted out his books at his locker.

"How was Austin's testosterone party?" Liz asked. She wheeled through her combination and snapped the locker open. "Have fun with the boys?"

Sam shrugged. "We ate pizza and played this new game, *The 13th Floor*."

"Never heard of it."

Sam grabbed his books and said, "Hardly anyone has. I guess it's banned in the States."

"Why?"

Sam shook his head. "It's just scary and gory. The only way you can play is if someone gets ahold of a pirated copy."

Austin leaned into the lockers between them. "Hazmat? You dating G.I. Jane here or what?"

"No, he is not!" Liz said.

Austin laughed. "At ease, soldier." Liz slammed her locker door and left in a huff. "What's her problem?"

"I don't know. What's up?"

Austin reached into his letterman jacket and pulled out a clear game case.

Sam took it hesitantly. "You're going to let me borrow it?"

"Borrow it, no." Austin smiled. "Tater scored us all copies."

"Sweet."

"I know," Austin said. "It's so addicting. I played it for like twelve hours straight." He yawned. "It's like I couldn't help myself. Still haven't recovered."

Sam flipped the case in his hands. "Did you get to the thirteenth floor?"

Austin shook his head. "I had trouble finding my way around the first floor."

"It's that hard?"

"Excruciating," Austin said. "But you can't help but want to figure it out. It's like it's a puzzle that you just have to solve."

The bell rang. Students darted off to class.

"Catch you later, Hazmat."

✦ ✦ ✦ ✦ ✦

When he got home that afternoon, Sam nuked a couple of burritos and went down to the basement. Munching on his dinner, he inserted the disc into his gaming system. Like the other night at Austin's, the system hummed oddly. Then the high-pitched squeal. Halfway through his first burrito, the lights in the house flashed. They went out with a sharp *plink*. The television came to life. The face of the doctor pushed through the murk. The dark goggles. The ceramic stork-beak mask. Again the face looked to the left, then the right. Behind the doctor, in the darkness, water dripped, echoing through the sanitarium.

"I am the doctor," the voice said. "But you already know that. I've seen your mind. Your innermost fears. Your lies. The darkness that slides across your soul. The game is quite simple. Find me before you go insane."

Sam didn't realize he had stopped chewing.

When the lights turned back on, the doctor had again stepped into the shadows.

Sam grabbed his controller and began playing. He checked the front desk, just like Johnny had. He picked up everything he could and read every scrap of paper. He moved to the bathroom in the hall. Checked all the toilet stalls. Wary of the doctor behind him, Sam kept turning around. But no doctor. He checked the other end of the hall. A women's bathroom.

All the mirrors were broken. The flickering fluorescent lights on the screen didn't bother him at first, but after a while, his head hurt.

He pushed on.

For hours, Sam braved the flickering lights, the blood smears on the floor, and the mysterious drips of water. Even the faint shuffling from behind the walls. He slowly pieced together the story thanks to the messages and journals he had found in rooms. An insane doctor experimented on his patients, and when the authorities went to the sanitarium to arrest him, all the police got lost and were eventually driven insane. As generations of family members came to the sanitarium to find their lost loved ones, they too got lost.

Sam's eyes grew tired, but he kept going.

He found a door with a small rectangular window.

When he looked through it, someone on the other side looked back at him.

"Jeez!" Sam dropped his controller in fright.

It took him a few moments to pick up the controller. Back in the game, he carefully approached the door again, worried the face would pop back up. But it didn't. Looking through the small window, he saw a table. On it lay a body under a bloody white sheet.

He tried the door. Locked. He picked up a nearby wrench and whacked at the window. Nothing. He looked around again, finding a bobby pin. He tried picking the lock. Nothing. Nothing seemed to work.

He had to get in. He had to know what was beyond the door. Maybe it held the secret to getting to the second floor.

He scavenged through all the rooms. There had to be something that could get him in. His mind was fluttering with ideas when his phone vibrated. Startled, Sam pulled it out of his jeans pocket. Austin. He answered it.

"Get into the locked room?"

"Not yet," Sam said. "You?"

"Yeah," Austin said. Then after a pause he added, "What I found was . . . Addicting, isn't it?"

"The game? Yeah."

"Let me know when you get through the door."

"Will do."

Sam put his phone away and continued. He approached the door again and peered through the window. Maybe something inside the room could provide a needed hint. The room was largely empty, except for the table and the body. There were blank, dingy walls to the left and to the right. Nothing on the floor. Nothing on the ceiling.

Wait. There was something on the ceiling. A vent near the left wall.

Sam turned around carefully, wary of the hiding doctor. He searched the nearby rooms, looking for another vent. It was three rooms down. He immediately began looking for a screwdriver or anything to help him remove the screws. A nail file! He removed the screws, threw back the vent cover, and pulled himself into the ventilation shaft above the room. Encased in darkness, he made his way around a few corners and through the shaft. Finally, he arrived over the locked room. Below him lay the bloodied body on the table. He kicked the vent until it fell to the floor with a crash.

Sam jumped down from the ventilation shaft. He approached the body and gripped the sheet. He peeled it off the body and saw the face of a woman. But it wasn't just any woman.

It was his mother.

Sam's heart lurched in his chest. He held his breath. Checked. Double-checked. It was his mom! What was she doing in the game? Sam couldn't take his eyes off the television. The fluttering lights flashed against his retinas. He had to move, get the image off the screen. He turned away from his mom's face. Behind him stood the doctor.

The dark goggles. The ceramic stork-beak mask. The bloodied white doctor's smock.

✦ ✦ ✦ ✦ ✦

"Sam," his father said, nudging his shoulder. Sam woke up on the couch in the basement. The controller had fallen to the floor. "Have you been playing all night?"

"What time is it?" Sam asked. He hadn't realized he had fallen asleep. His head pounded.

"Late, and it's a school night," his dad said. "Shut off the game and go to bed."

"Right," Sam said. He stood up and walked to the gaming console to turn it off, but it was already off.

Strange.

CHAPTER
5

Sam didn't want to admit it, but the game had him spooked. He couldn't sleep. Couldn't concentrate on school. He kept seeing that sheet being pulled off his mother's face. Then those goggles. The beak. The doctor.

At school, Austin and Mack appeared as slow and lethargic as Sam felt. And no one had seen Johnny at school all week.

At lunch, Sam got his tray of tacos and found the table in back where Austin and Mack sat. Sebastian and Harry from the glee club walked by, carrying their trays. Austin pointed a thumb at them and said, "Those turkeys wouldn't last an hour in this game."

"Hazmat," Mack said. "You look like I feel: exhausted."

Sam sat down and picked at his taco fixings. "Yeah. Where's Johnny? He hasn't been at school all week."

"Packing in an online marathon," Austin said. "You figure out that door?"

"The ventilation shaft," Sam said.

Mack nodded. Austin too. "What was on your table?" Austin asked.

Sam looked at him. His face twisted into a knot of confusion. "What do you mean? It was a woman." He didn't think they needed to know that he had seen his mother's face on the dead body in the game.

"No. I had an old man. My . . . grandfather," Mack said.

Sam looked at Austin. "What about you?"

Austin shook his head. "Bailey, my dog. He was hit by a car years ago."

Sam couldn't believe what he was hearing. Mack's grandfather. Austin's dog. His mother. How could a video game know about their own families, their pets?

"How can a game do that, use something from our past?" Sam wondered aloud.

Mack stuffed a taco in his mouth and said as he chewed, "It's all psychological, dude. We're just seeing things. They design it that way. To creep us out."

"Really?"

"Sure," Austin said. "What did you think of the second floor?"

Second floor? Sam hadn't played it since seeing his mother. "Never got to it."

Austin cut him a smile. "Scared?"

"No," Sam said right away. He didn't even know why he felt so defensive. "I've just had a lot of homework."

Mack laughed. "Homework. Right."

Sam wanted to tell them to shut up,
but he didn't. His head hurt. "What's on the
second floor?"

"More crazy stuff," Mack said. "But I don't
want to wreck it for you."

"Yeah," Austin said.

✦ ✦ ✦ ✦ ✦

After school, Sam fixed himself a peanut
butter and jelly sandwich for dinner. He wasn't
sure he wanted to play *The 13th Floor* anymore.
Not after what he had seen the other night. But
the house around him throbbed in silence. It
drummed in his ears. He turned on the television
to drown it out. Sports. Nothing. Movies.
Nothing. Cartoons. Nothing. No program on
any network held his interest.

Sam's gaming console stared back at him.

A black, plastic, faceless thing.

He had to see the second floor.

Sam grabbed a controller and turned on
the system. It booted, then lurched and hummed.

The screen came to life. Out of the blackness, the doctor loomed. "Back to test your fear?"

Sam wanted to answer him. Tell him he wasn't afraid.

"Good," the doctor said and walked back into the darkness.

The black screen opened up to his last saved progress: outside the locked door. He retraced his steps, working his way through the ventilation shaft and back into the room. The body lay on the table again. Same white sheet. Same blood stains. He walked about the room, conveniently ignoring the body. There was no other exit on the first floor. The locked room had to be the key. It was the gateway to the second floor. He searched all the walls, looking for anything he could pick up and use. Nothing. The only thing of interest was a poster hanging on the far wall. It was an anatomy poster of the human form. Over the abdomen was a circle painted in a fingertip of blood.

That had to be a clue. He examined the circled organ. The stomach. He reached out to touch the poster. It wavered at the bottom. The poster was only taped from the top. The bottom floated freely. He lifted the poster from the wall. Behind it was a keyhole. To a door. He only had to find the key. He turned around and scoured the room. There was no key to be found. The poster shuddered in the ventilated air. Sam looked at the red circle. The stomach.

The key is in the stomach, he realized. He lifted the sheet to reveal the desecrated body. The abdomen had been opened, revealing the grisly innards. Disgusted, he maneuvered his character over the body and dug through the organs until he found the key. Careful not to look at the woman's face, he turned away and unlocked the secret door. It creaked open on metallic hinges.

A cackling laughter came on over the sanitarium intercom system. "Congratulations," the doctor said. "You've made it to the second level of your madness."

The door opened to a stairway that led to the second floor. Sam navigated the stairs carefully, waiting for the doctor to sneak up behind him at any moment. A solitary lightbulb swung over his head, like someone or something had just bumped it. Scuffling footsteps rattled across the second floor.

Sam swallowed.

Onscreen, his character stepped to the top of the stairs. The swinging light slowed. When he got to the second floor, he a saw a mini tape recorder attached to the light's cord. Directly below it, sprawling across the floor, was the body of a man, his face frozen in fear.

Searching for clues was part of the game, so Sam checked the dead body: a pocketful of receipts, a wallet, a key chain, a pistol. He hit play on the tape recorder. Sam learned that the man was searching for his daughter, who was lost to the labyrinth of the asylum. The recording documented days, then weeks, of searching the building. His account grew manic, desperate, even depressed. During his last entry, the man wept uncontrollably. "She's gone!" he said. "Lost to the doctor. I have to join her."

Sam flipped through the wallet. Tom Beckett. He didn't recognize the name.

He continued to investigate the second floor. He found other victims. Some were the doctor's patients, others were searchers driven to their deaths by desperation.

Sam rubbed his eyes and looked at the clock. Quarter after ten. Had he really been playing that long already? Five hours? Time seemed to melt away. He looked out the basement window to get his bearings in the real world.

Onscreen, something bumped into a chair, and footsteps shuffled into the darkness. Sam snapped his attention back to the game. He followed the footsteps past several rooms, looking into each one. Patients littered the tables of each. Some surgically altered. Others had additional body parts sewn onto their bodies. One girl had her eyes, nose, and mouth stitched shut.

Sam understood why the game wasn't sold in the US. It was insane. No kid should ever play this thing. It was horrible.

The footsteps shuffled across the floor again. Sam swung his character around. Nothing. He saw a strobing light seeping through the crack underneath a door at the end of the hall. Sam felt a headache brewing, but he had to see what was behind the door. He made his character touch the doorknob, expecting it to be locked, but it wasn't. He flung the door open to reveal several shelves loaded with jars of yellow fluid. Objects floated in the liquid.

He investigated further, jar after jar. Some jars had baby booties suspended in the liquid. Others had lizards. Fingers. Eyes. Rows and rows of creepy stuff. The footsteps shuffled behind him, and a jar crashed to the floor. He turned around to see a wet human head on the ground.

He knew he shouldn't look. He was scared to see who it was. But at the same time, the anticipation was too great. Mack and Austin said he had to see it. He reached down, lifted up the head, and turned it over in his hands.

Liz.

He couldn't believe it. He looked again.

That was when the doctor said, "Don't get too close," and the game faded to black.

CHAPTER
6

Sam woke to darkness. Again. His phone vibrated in his pocket. Slow, steady, repeating. Not a text. A call. He quickly pulled it out of his pocket. 2:36 a.m. It was Mack. Sam answered.

"Where you been?!" Mack asked.

"Um, asleep." Sam's head hurt sharply. "Why, what's up?"

"Get over to Johnny's!"

"Why?"

"Just meet us there!"

Sam put on his shoes and dragged his bike out of the garage. Tired, he yawned as he pedaled over to Johnny's house. Twenty minutes later, he rounded the corner to flashing lights, an ambulance, and a police car in the driveway of Johnny's house. Sam dropped his bike and ran up the sidewalk to the front door. But before he could enter, two EMTs wheeled out a gurney with Johnny strapped to it. One of the EMTs pumped the airbag leading to Johnny's mouth.

Johnny's parents followed them out. His mother bawled loudly as his father wrapped his arm around her. Mack and Austin stood in the entryway of the house. After Johnny's father helped his wife into their car, he turned to Austin and said, "Can you stay at the house until the police officers leave?"

Austin and Mack nodded.

The two police officers asked the boys numerous questions about Johnny. *Did he do drugs? Had he ever made threats against himself or anyone else? Did he display any mentally ill behavior?* They answered no to pretty much everything. All three of them were more shocked than anything. After they left, Sam rubbed his head and asked, "What happened?"

45

Austin locked the front door and then said, "Come down here."

The three of them went downstairs to Johnny's room. As soon as Sam stepped in, he knew something was seriously wrong. It was a nightmare. Energy drink cans lay everywhere, accompanied by empty snack food wrappers. And the stink. It smelled like Johnny hadn't showered the whole week. But the worst of it was the drawings and the string. Johnny had pinned pictures of the characters from *The 13th Floor* all across his room, connecting them with red string. The boys had to duck under the crimson web to get into the room.

When Sam spun in a circle to take it all in, he noticed all the string led to one drawing, the doctor.

"What is all this?"

"The game," Mack said. "He was obsessed."

"He didn't try to . . . you know?"

"No," Austin said. "The EMTs said it looked like a combo of too many energy drinks and caffeine pills."

Sam shook his head. "This is crazy. The game caused this."

"Oh, come on," Austin scoffed.

"We have to get rid of the game," Mack said. "They find out he was playing a pirated video game and how he got it, and we'll all be in serious trouble."

"It was just getting good too," Austin whined.

Mack removed the disc from Johnny's gaming system and slid it into his coat pocket. "Go home and burn the discs. Get rid of them. I'll call Tater. Let him know to do the same. We're done. Out. This is too much."

✦ ✦ ✦ ✦ ✦

Sam rode his bike home in a fever. He ran downstairs, ejected the disc, then folded it in half until it broke. He folded each piece again and again until the game disc was a pile of small pieces. He went to the garage and grabbed a metal bucket and some lighter fluid. In the backyard, he put the pieces in the bucket, squirted them with lighter fluid, and dropped a lit match on top. When the disc was a bubbling mess of molten plastic on the bottom of the bucket, he sprayed the pail with the garden hose until the fire went out.

He went to bed, but he didn't sleep much.

He stared at his ceiling. His mother. Liz. Now Johnny.

How was all of this possible?

As tired as he felt, unanswered questions raced through his head. When he did finally fall asleep, his alarm immediately woke him for school.

He nodded off in the shower. In his cereal. On the bus ride to school. The bus driver had to wake Sam up to get him off the bus. In third period, he drooled over his algebra textbook.

Every time his eyes closed for a wink or two, he saw the doctor. The dark goggles. The ceramic stork-beak mask. He heard the muffled voice behind it. The laughter.

At lunch, he slid a dollar bill into the juice machine. The machine spit it out. He tried again. Rejection. Again, rejection.

"Argh," he huffed, kicking the machine.

"Don't let it get the best of you," Liz said. She walked over and took the dollar bill from his hands and fed it into the machine. Accepted. She slapped the apple juice button. After a few rumbles from the machine, she pulled out the bottle and handed it to Sam.

He looked at it. "I wanted orange."

"You looked like you needed less pulp." She looked around the cafeteria. It was oddly quiet. Just a dull hubbub. "What happened to Johnny?"

Sam thought about the game. His mother under the sheet. Liz's disembodied head. The shadows. The shuffling feet. The flickering lights. "The dummy chugged too many energy drinks. Fritzed out."

"The whole school is talking about it."

"Really?"

"Are you dense? The principal is going to talk about it in seventh period."

"Sorry," Sam said. "I haven't been sleeping well. I'm really tired."

"Well, wake up," she said. "Life is not like a video game, Sam. There is no reset button. No respawn. No do-overs."

At that point, he just wanted to tell her everything. The game. The creepy power outages. Johnny's obsession with it. Their cyber-bullying. The whole enchilada. But he heard Mack's voice in his head saying they could get into serious trouble, and he couldn't. "I know. I know," he muttered.

"Guys!" Liz said, shaking her head. "They're just monkeys in pants." She went off to lunch.

Sam took a sip of his juice and entered the cafeteria. He found Austin and Mack at a back table. Usually Mack ate one hot lunch and another cold lunch that his mom packed for him. He could pack it in. But today he just poked at his food. Austin wore sunglasses. An empty energy drink can sat next to him. A full can was gripped in his fist. Before Sam sat down, Austin took a long pull from the drink.

"What did Lara Croft want?" he asked.

Sam sat down and drank his juice. "Who?"

"Liz," Austin said. "Did you know she hunts with her father every fall? She sniped an elk in Colorado one year."

Sam nodded. "Really? Well . . . she's just trying to look out for me."

Off to the side, Mack had removed the top bun to his burger and was staring at the grayish patty of beef.

"What, need a girl to protect you?" Austin said. "That's rich."

"What's up with you?" Sam asked. "Johnny is messed up. Stop being a jerk."

"I can't help it that Johnny can't handle himself."

"You didn't look to be handling yourself all that well last night either." Next to them, Mack moved his face closer to the burger. "And quit drinking that junk," Sam continued.

Austin took another chug in defiance of Sam's advice. "What do you know, Hazmat? You'd be nothing in this school if we hadn't taken you in. Right, Mack?"

Mack didn't answer. He only stared at the landscape of his burger. His face was almost on top of it.

"Mack?"

No answer.

"Mack?"

Finally, Mack turned to them. "What?"

"What are you doing?" Austin asked. "You've been staring at your lunch for the last fifteen minutes."

Mack shook his head. "Just zoning out. Last night was crazy, dudes. Johnny looked whacked up. Did you dispose of yours?"

Austin held up his finger to his lips. "Shh, quiet. Jeez. Yes. Done."

Sam drank more juice. "Me too. Burned it with some lighter fluid."

"Pyro," Austin said.

"Shut up," Sam said. "We all agreed. We're out. Done. And good riddance if you ask me. That game was too much."

Austin laughed. "It got to you, didn't it?"

Sam didn't want to answer. He felt like his reputation with Austin was at stake. But Liz's voice whispered in his head and told him otherwise. *Who cares what a dumb football player thinks?* "Yes. It did."

Austin laughed.

Mack slapped Austin on the shoulder. "Don't ride him."

"Why not?" Austin said.

"It got to me too."

CHAPTER
7

Sam's father was waiting for him after school. "I thought we'd see a movie at the mall tonight," he said. "I've heard the one with alien monsters versus giant robots is pretty cool."

Sam's cell phone vibrated with a text message. He checked it, *Miss me?* But it was an unknown number. He stuffed the phone back into his pocket.

"Sure. A movie would be cool," he said.

"So what happened to this Johnny?"

Sam shook his head, remembering his promise. "Went on a gaming bender. Freaked out, I guess."

"I'm sorry," his dad said. "What about you? The games?"

"I'm taking a break," Sam said. "Time to be more productive in school."

"Good."

✦ ✦ ✦ ✦ ✦

In line at the concession stand, Sam asked to get a bag of gummy bears for the movie. It had been a tradition between him and his mom. She always got them for him, then snuck a few for herself once the movie had started.

"Sure," his dad said.

Sam's phone vibrated with a text again, *Hear what happened to Johnny?* The same unknown number.

"Shut that thing off for the movie," his dad said while paying for the snacks.

Sam nodded, then clicked off his phone and stowed it in his pocket.

The movie was everything the ads promised. Disgusting looking alien monsters and giant robots battling. One of the robots actually used a construction crane as a weapon. Outside the theater, Sam and his dad threw away their trash, and Sam turned his phone back on to check it.

Three more text messages from the unknown number.

Miss your mommy?

Where have you been hiding?

You need to finish.

Sam stopped walking through the mall. His dad was steps ahead of him before he realized Sam had stopped. "Is something wrong?"

Sam quickly shut off his phone and put it in his pocket. "No. Nothing's wrong. Just some crazy texts."

They continued out of the mall. Most shops had closed up for the night. Sam thought back to the texts, fear coursing through his veins.

He thought about the game. How could it be connected to those texts? He had destroyed the disc just last night. Austin had to be messing with him. Their confrontation in the school cafeteria must have gotten to Austin. He needed to lash out, put Sam back in his place.

That had to be it.

They walked past an electronics store. It was dark inside. But as Sam walked by, the tablets and laptops all powered on. A dull glow lit the screens. A face pressed through the blackness. The dark goggles. The white ceramic stork-beak mask. The doctor. A laugh cackled through the store.

Sam pointed and croaked to his dad, "Did you see that?"

But before his dad could turn to look, the screens went black again.

"See what?"

Sam bit a fingernail.

✦ ✦ ✦ ✦ ✦

The ride home was torture. Sam had to check. He had to be sure that he had broken the disc and burned it into a puddle of melted plastic. Or had he just imagined it? He remembered the headaches. The power outages. The epileptic frenetic lighting in the game. His dreary sleepiness. Had the game done that? Had he spent so much time playing it that it actually screwed up his mind? He thought about Johnny. The EMTs. The drawings in his basement. The red string. Johnny was trying to figure something out, and it drove him insane. Just like the game said it would.

Sam bolted out of the car and ran into the house before his dad had a chance to turn off the ignition in the driveway. He took the downstairs steps two at a time. At the television, Sam pressed the eject button on the gaming system. It took forever processing, and in that time a fear grew in his mind like a weed in cracked pavement. Another disc was going to be in the console. He knew it. Someone was messing with him.

But when the console opened up, there was nothing inside.

CHAPTER
8

Sam sat in the food court at the mall and furiously bit his fingernails. One finger had started bleeding. He hadn't slept at all the night before, and he didn't dare use his cell phone or his computer. Not even the television. It was maddening being unplugged. Boring. Quiet. It made him think way too much. Especially on all the things they were dealing with. He even called Austin and Mack from the landline phone in his kitchen.

He looked at his old Transformers watch. They were late. The rubber watchband felt awkward on his wrist. He never wore it anymore now that he had a smartphone. Sam's head hurt.

His eyes drooped. He'd kill for a restful night's sleep again.

"Hazmat," Austin said from behind him. He rounded the table and sat down across from Sam. He set down a plate with a huge slice of sausage pizza. "What's up with the cloak and dagger crap? Why didn't you just tell me over the phone?"

"I had to be sure," Sam said. "Where's Mack?"

"I'm not his keeper. I'm sure he'll show," Austin said. "What do you have to be sure about?"

"Are you screwing with me?" Sam asked.

"Screwing with you? What do you mean?"

"I got a bunch of texts last night from an unknown number. About the game."

"So?"

"Did you send them?"

"No. Why would I do that?"

"Then it must be the game," Sam muttered.

"What?"

"The doctor. He's messing with us."

"From the game?"

"Yeah," Sam said. "The texts were taunting me, telling me to finish the game. And when I walked by the electronics store last night, even though the store was closed, all the laptops and tablets powered on just for me. Again, the doctor."

"That's crazy."

"So, you haven't experienced any of that? Any creepy stuff?"

Austin ate his pizza and laughed. He shook his head and sat still for a few moments, lost in thought. "It can't all be from the game, Sam. Can it? How's that possible?"

The sound of crackling voices interrupted Sam's train of thought. Nearby, a mall security guard briefly held a walkie-talkie to his ear before hurrying across the food court into the main part of the mall.

"Maybe the doctor caused what happened to Johnny. Maybe he was getting harassed too, so he tried to finish the game."

"That's nuts, Sam," Austin said.

Another security guard passed by on the run.

"Never seen a rent-a-cop run like that before," Austin said.

A yell came from across the mall. The boys turned to see what was going on. A second later, four police officers ran past the food court, heading in the same direction as the mall security guards.

Sam stood up. "What's going on?"

Austin stood too. "Let's check it out."

Both boys ran behind the police. The yelling got louder. They couldn't make out what was being said, but it sounded desperate, even manic.

The ruckus was coming from the electronics store. The police officers had formed a perimeter outside its entrance.

Austin and Sam stopped in their tracks.

There in the middle of the store stood Mack, smashing computer after computer. The store clerks cowered behind displays.

"He's in them all!" Mack yelled.

He smashed a tablet against the wall. Cracked smartphones and broken computers were now rubble at his feet.

"Put your hands on your head and lie down on the floor!" yelled one of the police officers.

Mack paused mid-destruction. "You don't understand!" he yelled. "He's everywhere. Computers. Phones. My head." Mack pointed to his head. "He won't stop until I finish the game! But I can't. I destroyed it."

Mack grabbed a nearby computer and raised it above his head. One of the police officers stepped into the store and fired a Tazer

at Mack. Juiced with electricity, Mack shook
in place. The laptop slipped from his fingers as
Mack fell to the floor in convulsions. A couple of
police officers were on him in no time, wrestling
him into position. Another police officer zip-tied
Mack's hands behind his back and read him
his rights.

"Oh, wow," Austin gasped.

Sam grabbed him by the jacket and pulled
him back around the corner. "Still think it's
some kind of prank?"

"No. What do we do?"

"Lie low," Sam said. "No gaming, no
phone, no computer. Go to school, play football.
Move on."

"This is all crazy, Sam. Johnny and now
Mack. What's in that game?"

"I don't know," Sam said. "I don't know."

CHAPTER
9

Sam stayed in his room for the rest of the day. He kept his cell phone turned off and left it on his desk.

He grabbed a book off his shelf. *1984* by George Orwell. He was two pages into it when his laptop screen shuddered to life by itself. The doctor's face came into view.

Sam shut the laptop.

He went downstairs and grabbed a glass of ice water with shaking hands. His head hurt again. He wanted to sleep, but his mind wouldn't let him. Sam stared across the kitchen. The digits on the microwave clock flashed before being replaced by a scrolling message. He squinted, hoping it said something about shutting the door or continuing the cook cycle.

Finish the game.

Sam walked over to the microwave and pressed all the buttons. But only the time displayed.

"Hey, son," his dad said from behind him.

Sam let out a high-pitched gasp and nearly dropped his glass.

"Oh, sorry. Didn't mean to frighten you. How was the mall?"

"Fine."

Behind his father, the television came to life. The doctor loomed out of the darkness wheeling a gurney. Sam was so exhausted, he didn't know if he was seeing things or not. But it looked like his dad lay on the gurney. His abdomen was open, exposing all his insides.

"You look exhausted," his father said. "Get some rest."

Sam wished it were that easy. He walked back upstairs to his room. He rolled onto his bed and closed his eyes. The room began to spin behind his closed lids. He swore he heard scurrying feet on the roof. Behind the walls, he heard scratching and slow, sad sobbing.

It was all a trick.

All in his mind.

None of it was real.

He hoped.

✦ ✦ ✦ ✦ ✦

"Son," his father said, shaking him awake.

Sam rolled over. His mouth was dry. The ache in his head was gone. The weariness behind his eyes had disappeared. He felt refreshed. Rested. Like everything that had happened, hadn't. "What time is it?"

"Three o'clock."

"That was a really great nap."

"It's Sunday, Sam," his father said. "You must have been tired. You slept for twenty-seven hours."

"No way!" Sam said.

"Sam, I woke you because you have a visitor."

"A visitor?"

"Yes. A girl. Liz Fallon?"

"What does she want?"

"I don't know," he said. "She's waiting downstairs."

"Okay. Okay."

Sam changed his clothes and went downstairs. Liz sat at the nook in the kitchen. Stretching his arms above his head, he walked into the kitchen and said, "Liz. What's up?"

"I thought I'd check in with you."

Sam got out some cereal and poured himself a bowl. "You hungry?"

Liz shook her head. "How have you been lately?"

Sam poured milk onto his cereal. "Fine. Just had a really good sleep."

"I'm just worried about you. First Johnny, then Mack. Now Austin."

Mid-bite, Sam said, "Austin?"

"Have you not seen the news?"

Sam rubbed his temple. The dull ache returned. "No. Been trying to stay unplugged lately. Screen overload."

Liz reached over to the television and turned it on. The local news was in mid-broadcast. A reporter stood in a cornfield. The text on the bottom of the screen read: Missing Local Boy Found in Field. The reporter talked about how police had found him in the middle of the night in just his underwear.

"The only discernible clue to what happened," the reporter said, "was the writing on the boy's body. The phrase 'Finish the game!'

had been written all over his body in black permanent marker. As the starting linebacker for the high school football team, investigators are looking into possible hazing as the cause. Regardless, local authorities will get to the bottom of the mystery."

Sam just stared at the television.

"Do you know what's going on?"

Sam's stomach turned. He wanted to throw up right there. He was the last one. Johnny. Mack. Austin. Only he remained. He bit a fingernail and looked at Liz.

"If I tell you, you can't tell anyone else."

Liz nodded.

Sam moved and sat down next to her. He told her everything. Their online bullying of other gamers, some of them students at their school. Austin's montage of gaming videos. Their *Warpath* online parties. Then he told her about *The 13th Floor*. That it wasn't legal in the States. That a kid named Tater pirated it and gave them all a copy. He described the game in great detail. The doctor. The gameplay. The horrific imagery. His mother. Everything except the part about Liz's head. He told her that Johnny had gone mad trying to finish the game. How they destroyed their game discs. Unplugged. Then Mack went bananas in the electronics store.

"And now Austin," Liz finished.

"Yes," Sam said. "We made a pact to stop playing."

"He obviously didn't listen."

"Yeah."

"So what do we do?"

Sam took a deep breath and shook his head. "We have to finish the game."

"But you burned your disc," Liz said. "All of you."

That didn't seem to matter. Sam got up and walked to the basement. "Come with me."

"Why?"

"I have a funny feeling I need to check out."

They walked down into the basement. Sam turned on the lights, then walked over to his gaming console and turned it on. The unit cycled to life as the television screen flickered on. Just as Sam suspected, the game loaded even without the disc. The doctor's face pushed out of the darkness.

"Hello, Sam," the doctor said almost pleasantly.

"How can the game work without a disc?" Liz asked. "How does it know your name?"

"The game downloaded itself onto the hard drive, I bet," Sam said.

"Finish the game," the doctor said onscreen. "It's the only way out."

"Not before I get a few things," Sam said.

"What things?" Liz asked.

CHAPTER
10

"Thanks, Mrs. Keller," Sam said. He and Liz stood on the stoop to the Keller house. He held a box of Johnny's pictures and notes about the game.

Mrs. Keller dabbed her eyes. "Just take them. They're horrible, horrible pictures." She paused. "And I don't want them around if gaming drove him to it."

He and Liz both looked down at their feet. Then with a whispered good-bye, they left.

✦ ✦ ✦ ✦ ✦

Back at Sam's house, they made some pizza rolls and grabbed a bunch of sodas. In the basement, they ate while Sam looked over Johnny's notes. Liz shuddered. "How can you eat and look at this stuff?"

"I'm hoping it'll keep my blood sugar up. Reduce the headaches."

"Headaches," Liz said. "The game does that to you?"

Sam nodded. He paged through the drawings and pages of notes. Johnny had made it to level 12. He had written down all the clues, puzzles, locations, and solutions. Sam was on his own after that.

He grabbed his controller and turned to Liz. "You ready?"

She nodded.

"You need to stay awake. Monitor me. If I start to wig out like the others, stop me, whatever you need to do. I can't let the game get to me. Got it?"

"Got it."

Sam entered the game where he'd left off, Liz's disembodied head rolling across the floor.

She gasped. "That's me! How am I in the game?"

"I'm not really sure," Sam admitted.

In the game, Sam reached down and held the head. From Johnny's notes, he knew to check inside the mouth, where he found a wet piece of paper with a four-digit code written on it. It was a keypad code. Sam searched the entire floor until he found the keypad next to a door. He punched in the code, and the door opened to the third level.

The door to the stairway shut tightly behind him. Water dripped everywhere, and the sound of gushing water could be heard in the distance. His footsteps sloshed about as he tried to navigate around the dead bodies floating in the water. Sam looked at Johnny's notes. The room was flooding. He had to find the next floor before drowning. He paged through the notes. The only thing he could find was the word *blow*.

Blow? What did that mean? Back in the game, he searched and searched. Meanwhile, the water level rose. Worse, the screen shuddered as his character was bit by something unseen. Blood frothed in the water. Piranhas swam around his legs. He half ran, half swam as he searched for a clue. Door after door, he found nothing. Finally, he spotted a door with a hole in it and a pressure gauge above it.

But he was too late. The water was above his head, and the piranhas swarmed.

"Too late," the doctor said.

"This game is sick," Liz said. "No wonder it's been banned."

Sam restarted the third level, this time understanding Johnny's cryptic notes. Blow. The door was activated by breathing into it. He rushed through the level, swatting at the fish in the water. The water rose higher and higher. By the time he got to the door, he was completely submerged. He put his face to the hole in the door and blew. The longer he blew, the whiter the screen got until his character passed out.

His avatar awoke on the fourth floor.

Sam checked the notes. *Bugs.* The fourth floor was all about bugs. Johnny's notes said the only way out was through a massive pit of insects. He found the pit and jumped in. The bugs bit and stung his onscreen character. Green splotches oozed along the outer edge of the screen, signifying the amount of poison the bugs had injected into him. He died before reaching the key.

He retried the scenario. This time he found an old fire extinguisher and blasted the pit with it. He unloaded the whole canister on the swarm until they crawled out of the pit. At the bottom was a red button that unlocked the door to the fifth floor.

Liz screamed and jumped off the couch. "A freaking spider was on my neck." She swatted at herself, jerkily dancing across the floor.

"Take it easy," Sam said. "Don't let it get to you. It's all in your head."

"I felt it, Sam. I felt it."

Sam shook his head and continued. Using Johnny's notes, it was easy to navigate the levels. Level five was fire. His character had to get through the fifth floor before burning to death. It took him three tries to get through it. His head throbbed as the flames swirled before him hypnotically. Level six was snakes, tons of them. He stopped midway through the level and moved to the other side of couch, closer to Liz. He felt a slithering through his hair but didn't want to say anything and freak her out.

The seventh floor was set to a timer. The air was gradually being sucked out of the building, and he had to figure out the puzzle before suffocating. The edge of the screen grew darker and darker as his character's oxygen levels dwindled, but he made it.

Floor eight was ghosts. Floor nine, blindness. Sam had to navigate the entire floor in the dark. It didn't help either that the lights in the basement went out for that entire level. On the tenth floor was a horde of zombies. He spent an hour trying to survive their attacks. It took him nine restarts to get it right.

Sam's eyes grew weary. He checked the clock. Two in the morning. But he had to push through. Next to him, Liz had dozed off. He nudged her awake.

"You can't fall asleep."

"Aren't you finished yet?"

Sam shook his head and continued. Level 11 was probably the most disturbing. The whole floor was covered with numerous victims who had been butchered. Blood covered the walls. Sam's stomach turned. He burped and fought back the bile in his throat.

Again, Liz had fallen asleep.

He soldiered through. On the final door, a sign read, "One bowl to pass."

THE 13TH FLOOR

A small table held a bowl of vile stew that looked like it had fingers floating in it. Sam sat his character down and ate the bowl of stew. The door opened, and he advanced to the twelfth floor. Unlike all the other levels, this one had no other rooms. No dead bodies. No gore or horror. No bugs or snakes. It was just a room with an expansive glass wall and a door that led to the edge of the roof. Something was written in blood along the outer ledge. Sam moved his character closer. The bloody words spelled "The 13th Floor."

There was nowhere else to go but over the edge. The thirteenth floor wasn't a floor at all. It was the pavement below.

"Finish it," the doctor's voice said.

Liz was right. The game was twisted. To finish, to get to the thirteenth floor, his character had to leap over the edge. Sam put down his controller and rubbed his eyes. A yawn escaped his mouth. This was the place where Johnny lost it. Then Mack. Austin too. All of them had been driven insane by the game. Had they advanced

to the thirteenth floor? Did access to that final
level make them crazy?

His eyes heavy, Sam picked up the
controller and moved his character to the edge.
He held his breath as the world around him—the
couch, the carpet, a softly snoring Liz—melted
away. Nothing real existed anymore. Sam was
in the game. His feet shuffled to the edge of
the roof. His heart raced. His brow dripped
with sweat. He couldn't do it. Whether it was a
game or not, he couldn't take that final step. He
wouldn't give in to it.

But there was no other way to get to the
end. He pushed the stick forward and fell. His
eyes heavy, his head throbbing, he fell to the
thirteenth floor. Sam watched the spiraling
blackness and waited to hit the pavement. But he
didn't. Only a sprawling darkness stretched to
infinity before him. Then, out of the blackness,
the white outline of a backlit door took shape.
It creaked open, revealing an address: 333
Horsham Street.

"Congratulations," the doctor said. "You've found me."

Sam rubbed his eyes. That was it? An address?

Then it hit him. The address was real. It was downtown.

As if the game had read his mind, the doctor said, "I can't wait to meet you. There's a car waiting for you outside."

"Are you going to kill me?"

The doctor laughed. "If I had intended to do that, would I have gone through all this trouble?" Onscreen, the doctor turned and walked into the blackness. "Besides, you want to know the truth. Come alone. Leave the girl to her dreams."

Sam looked over at Liz curled up on the couch next to him.

He had to go.

CHAPTER
11

The drive into the city took a long time. The driver didn't say a word, even when Sam asked him questions.

He shouldn't have gotten in the car. He should have stayed at home. With Liz. But at the same time, if he didn't figure out why this had happened, Johnny, Mack, and Austin would have suffered for nothing. No. He needed to complete the game.

The car stopped outside a 30-story skyscraper. Sam didn't wait for instructions. He got out and walked to the front door. The car idled in place. He entered through the revolving door. A front desk sat unattended. A logo hung above it: *Lucidity Software*.

THE 13TH FLOOR

He walked to the elevator bay. A directory on the wall showed that Lucidity was the only occupant of the building. On the thirteenth floor. An open elevator waited for him. Sam stepped into it and went to find the button, but there was only one: 13.

He pressed it.

The lights flickered all the way up.

Finally the elevator dinged and the doors opened. The thirteenth floor was blindingly bright. Sam held up a hand to shade his eyes. Stepping forward, he noticed a medicinal smell to the room, like the dentist's office.

"Ah," the doctor's voice resonated. "You made it."

Sam put down his hand and let his eyes get adjusted to the light. The entire floor was open. No interior walls. He couldn't even see where the light was coming from. But there stood the doctor behind a glass divider. Gone was his bloodied smock from the game. Instead he wore a black pinstriped suit and black leather gloves.

The black goggles and the ceramic stork-beak mask over his face were the only things that remained the same.

"What's that odor?" Sam said.

The doctor nodded. "Nitrous oxide. A diluted mix." He looked at his watch. "We have about twenty minutes before you drift off to sleep."

Sam shook his head. "Always with the games. I figured it out, you know."

The doctor nodded. "Of course you did. The disc was a Trojan horse. Once the game disc booted, it infected your system. Gave me access to . . . everything. Gamers always have the best bandwidth, and they all own smartphones and computers. Even alarm systems and power grids are hooked into the Internet nowadays.

"Once I was in, I could see social profiles. Legal documents. Phone records. User IDs. Passwords. Pictures of Mommy. Daddy. Friends. But that was just the logistical heavy lifting."

"The headaches," Sam said. His head felt woozy, his eyelids heavy. "What did you do to us?"

"Did you know a quickly flashing light at just the right frequency can cause seizures?" The doctor paced back and forth behind the glass. "Certain ambient sounds trigger precise emotions and reactions. Subliminal imagery shown at a fraction of frame speed can suggest thoughts and actions. They are all part the game. With the right combination of triggers, I can get any one person to do my bidding. And the really fun part is they don't even know they're doing it. To them, they're just losing their minds as they can't stop playing my game."

Sam felt his legs get wobbly. He was turning numb. His eyelids blinked heavy and slow. "You're a monster," he said thickly.

The doctor shook his head, his beak wavering slow and steady. "Me? A monster? Hardly. I've seen you and your friends online. How you treat others. The video montages.

The bullying. Perhaps you should rethink your definition of the word *monster*."

"What is this, then, revenge?"

The doctor shook his head at Sam. "Oh, no, no, no. I choose to think of it as an educational exercise. No. What I've done here is create a valuable teaching tool. Did you know close to two thousand kids commit suicide each year to relieve their pain from bullying? Quadruple that number, and that's how many kids attempt it and fail. No. This masterpiece is to teach you and your ilk of the pain you inflict on others every day. Your ordeal is nothing compared to what others and their families have to endure!"

It was the only time Sam had heard the doctor get emotional. The anger in his voice made Sam want to barf all over the white room. Like a tree ready to topple, he lurched unsteadily on his feet. "Why did you bring me here?"

The doctor collected himself, straightening his tie and interlocking his hands behind his back. "Your role is quite simple. I need you to tell this story. Stand up against the very things you and your friends have done. That's all I ask. Nothing more. If you ask me, it's a small price to pay considering all that's happened."

"But they'll never believe me," Sam said. "They'll think I'm crazy."

The doctor turned his head to the side, displaying the profile of the horrible stork-beak mask. "I'm counting on that. Only the truly twisted, crazy stories get told. Retold. Burned into the retinas of legend. You won't be telling a story as much as being part of one."

Sam wasn't quite sure what that meant, but there was something he needed to know, "What's your name?"

The doctor turned away from Sam and walked into the bright whiteness in the distance. Sam fought against the drug, using all his strength to keep his eyes and ears open. When the doctor had almost vanished completely into the blinding light, he said, "Doctor Matthew Bernard Dellapest."

Sam closed his eyes.

✦ ✦ ✦ ✦ ✦

"Sam!" his father called.

Sam opened his eyes. A jagged lightning bolt of pain arched through his head. The front of his shirt stuck wetly to his chest. His father knelt over him in his pajamas, shaking him in terror. Behind his father, Liz stood against the wall, crying. When his father saw Sam's eyes open, he said, "Sam! You're okay. When Liz woke me, I thought the worst. You scared me, son."

Sam shook his head and sat up. He had been lying on the floor. "Why is my shirt wet?"

Liz sniffled and said, "You started foaming at the mouth. Your eyes rolled back and you collapsed. I thought it was a seizure."

"What?" Sam said. "That's impossible. I was downtown. I figured out the game. He sent a car to pick me up. I met the doctor. He told me everything."

His father shook his head. "Game?"

"Yeah. A weird game that my friends gave me. It made them all go crazy, but I figured it out. I met the doctor!"

Liz shook her head. "No, you didn't. I was with you the whole time, Sam. You told me to watch you. That if you started acting funny, I needed to snap you out of it. But I couldn't. You just stopped playing and sat there. Then you started shaking. You wouldn't wake up, so I got your dad."

Sam rubbed his head. "No. That's not true. I saw him. He told me I had to tell everyone. To change things. To stop bullying wherever I saw it. I even figured out his name!"

"Who?" his father asked.

"The doctor," Sam said. "The man in the video game. The doctor. He's Matty Dellapest. The kid they named the antibullying policy at school for. He's the doctor. He made the game as a lesson to us. Matty Dellapest did all of this."

"No," Liz said. "He couldn't."

"I'm telling you, it's him!"

"Sam, it's impossible. Matty Dellapest's dead. That's why they made the rule. A bunch of football players bullied him. He jumped out a window at his dad's office building. He couldn't have done all this, Sam. He's dead."

"That's not right," Sam said. His headache flared up again. "That can't be. I saw him. He told me everything. That's not possible."

Sam's father helped him stand up. "I think it's best that we get you to a doctor and make sure you're okay."

Sam nodded numbly. He still didn't believe it. Everything had felt so real. He followed his father out of the basement. Before he went too far, Liz leaned into him and hugged him tightly. "It's going to be okay, Sam."

"You have to believe me. It's the truth! I'm not crazy! I'm not crazy! The doctor didn't win!"

About the Author

Scott Welvaert has published numerous titles,
including two middle grade fantasy adventure
novels: *The Curse of the Wendigo* and *The Mosquito
King*. His book of poetry, *Pacific*, won the Sol
Books Award and was subsequently published
through Skywater Publishing. He graduated with
an M.F.A. in Creative Writing and currently
lives in Minnesota with his wife, two daughters,
and a dog named Sparrow.

Questions to Think About

1. Sam and his friends can't stop playing *The 13th Floor*. As you learn at the end of the story, that is because of the way the game was programmed. Have you ever been obsessed with something, whether it was playing a game or eating a certain type of food? What caused this obsession and how did you get over it?

2. Sam's new friends, Austin, Johnny, and Mack, like to harass people in the online gaming world. Do you think online bullying is any different from bullying people in the real world? Why or why not?

3. Imagine you are a character in your favorite game. Describe the game and what you are like while in this game. Then write a story about how you work your way through the game. Be sure to describe the types of obstacles that you have to defeat and explain how you beat them.

The Squadron

Sera has a chance to join an elite group of space pilots. All she needs to do is complete one flight, from the Old World to the New Colonies. But damage to one of her engines sends her off course. She crashes onto a violent dwarf planet with a molten core that is slowly devouring its surface. And that might be the least of her worries.

THREE CHORDS AND A BEAT

Joey's brother, Trey, died several months ago, and things aren't getting any easier for him. Joey's newfound anger leads to a fight at school that results in him being expelled. Looking for answers to his brother's death and his own issues, Joey finds his brother's guitar. Could the old guitar provide the answers Joey seeks?

THE WISH

Before a fight with the strongest kid in school, Robert wishes for a miracle that would save his face from being turned into a bloody pulp and change everything about the world he lives in. When his wish is granted, Robert quickly learns that the new world it created comes with its own set of problems.

READ MORE FROM 12-STORY LIBRARY
Every 12-Story Library book is available in many formats, including Amazon Kindle and Apple iBooks. For more information, visit your device's store or 12StoryLibrary.com.